The Twins Strike Back

by
Valerie Flournoy

illustrated by
Melodye Rosales

For my twin sister and best friend, Vanessa,
who always wanted to have the last laugh.

ISBN 0-940975-52-1 (Paperback)   0-940975-51-3 (Hardcover)
Library of Congress Cataloging in Publication Number 94-76813
Printed in the U.S.A.
12 11 10 9 8 7 6 5 4 3 2 1

Natalie and Nicole raced each other down Arch Street. At the end of the block they could see their older sister, Bernadine, and their cousin Nate playing ball with some of their friends.

"Oh, brother," Nicole wailed. "Trouble."

"Well, well, well," Nate said as the twins attempted to pass by the group quickly, "if it isn't Pete and Repeat or should I call you two Bip and Bop?"

Natalie and Nicole looked at one another and sighed.

1

Bernadine and her friends burst into laughter.

"You know our names, Nate," Natalie said, glaring.

"Ignore him, Nat" Nicole said. "You know the old saying—"

"Empty boxes make the most noise," the twins said together.

"See, they even say the same thing at the same time," Nate howled. "Twins are definitely weird!"

"Why don't you go play in traffic?" Natalie said.

"Yeah, take a hike," added Nicole and without another word the two girls ran up the front steps and shut the door behind them."

"Mom! We're home!" Natalie yelled.

"Where are you?" Nicole added. "Nate's at it again."

The two girls stomped through the house into the kitchen.

"Ssh . . . quiet!" Mother scolded. "I'm on the phone with your grandfather."

Nicole opened the refrigerator for a glass of milk, while Natalie searched for the last can of her favorite black cherry soda.

"I'm sorry, Dad," Mother said. "As I was saying, Natalie got a B in math and Nicole got a D. If one twin can get a B, why can't the other? I just don't understand the twins."

Nicole jumped from her chair and marched out the back door.

Her glass of milk forgotten. "I hate numbers!" she muttered. "And my name is Nicole . . . not twins."

"Now what's the matter with her?" Mother asked.

Natalie found her sister on the seesaw their father had made for them.

"Don't let it get you down," Natalie said, sitting on the other end. "You know Mom knows our names. Sometimes it's just easier to say twin instead of Natalie and Nicole."

"Yeah, but what about if you can get a B so should I," Nicole asked.

"Well, maybe Mom doesn't know that I like math and you don't," Natalie sighed and for a while the two girls seesawed up and down in silence.

"Hey, twins!" Bernadine called as she and Nate ran into the backyard. "My team's one person short. Do you guys want to play?"

"No, thanks," Nicole sighed.

"Not interested," agreed Natalie.

4

Bernadine sat on the grass next to the seesaw. "How come you twins are so grouchy when tomorrow's your birthday?"

Nicole and Natalie looked at one another and refused to answer.

"So tomorrow's your birthday, huh? I can't believe you two will be older than me," Nate said slyly.

Now it was Nicole's turn to laugh. "You are dumb, Nate. Nat and I will only be eight tomorrow, and you're almost eleven."

"That's right. But if you 're gonna be eight and Natalie's gonna be eight too, well, then, it's simple—you're older because eight and eight is—"

"Sixteen," Natalie supplied eagerly.

Nicole jumped off the seesaw, sending Natalie crashing to the ground. "Oh, you and your math!" she said to her twin. "And you and your stupid jokes, Nate!"

5

Nate and Bernadine rolled in the grass, laughing hysterically.

"Boy, I don't feel too well," groaned Natalie. "And, I didn't mean to show off by adding those numbers."

"Yes, I know," Nicole muttered, helping her sister to the house. "But even though you're my best friend, I sometimes wish people would just see me . . . for me. Understand?

Natalie thought for a moment. "Like the time you won the library reading contest and I wasn't even among the top ten winners.

"Exactly," beamed Nicole.

"Instead of people being happy for you," Natalie remembered. "Everyone wondered why I hadn't won too."

Even with the kitchen door closed, Natalie and Nicole could still hear Nate's laughter as Bernadine told all their friends about his joke.

"One of these days," Natalie muttered.

"Yeah, one of these days *we* are gonna have the last laugh on those two," Nicole vowed. "You'll see."

That night Natalie and Nicole helped their father clear the dinner dishes, while Mother washed them and Bernadine dried.

"Tomorrow there's a double horror-thriller at the movie matinee," Bernadine said as she put the plates away," and all my friends will be going. Do the twins have to tag along?"

Father smiled at Bernadine and nodded. "Tomorrow is the twins' birthday, and they want to go to the movies and be scared to death too. So I don't want to hear another word about them going."

"And another thing," Mother added. "When you see your friends, tell them to leave the twins alone and quit treating them as if they're from outer space."

"But they are," Bernadine said, sulking. "They dress alike and they probably even think alike too and—s

"Not another word," Father warned. "It's settled."

"We're finished," Nicole said.

"And another wonderful job too," said Father.

The two girls raced upstairs to their room. Nicole flopped on her neatly made bed while Natalie tried to find an empty spot on her cluttered bed to sit down.

"So Bernadine thinks we're from outer space," Nicole said angrily, "and that we think alike too!"

An devilish look crossed Natalie's face. "Why, of course we think alike."

Nicole stared at her sister. "Maybe that fall off the seesaw hurt you more than you thought."

"No, it didn't, silly," said Natalie, "but if Bernadine already *thinks* we can read each other's minds anyway—"

"Then it should be simple for us to convince her that she's absolutely right," Nicole added, thinking of all the possibilities. "And we can get Fish to help us."

Fish was Nicole and Natalie's best friend. Everyone called him Fish because he liked to swim. To him any nickname was better than his real name—Woodrow.

"Come on," said Natalie. "Let's phone Fish now."

The next morning Father and Mother left the house early to go shopping. "Don't eat too much at the movies," Father said.

"Yes, save some room for cake and ice cream at Grandma and Grandpa's this evening," Mother put in. "And have a terrific birthday movie and day, girls."

"Oh, we will," Natalie said slyly. "We will."

Natalie and Nicole returned to their room to perfect their plan and work on their timing. Then Nicole kept lookout while Natalie phoned Fish to remind him to be at the park at three o'clock.

"Twins, Nate's here!" Bernadine yelled. "Are you two gonna stay upstairs all day?"

"We'll be right down," Nicole yelled back.

"Now, I'll leave my sneakers here," Natalie whispered. "Give me five minutes and don't forget what we practiced." She ran quickly down the stairs.

"Well, its about time," Bernadine said as she finished setting the breakfast table.

"Nate's mom said he could have breakfast with us this morning."

"Yeah," said Nate, "but by the time you twins get to the table, it'll be lunchtime." He sat at the table and poured milk over his cereal. "By the way, which are you? Doctor Jekyll or Miss Hyde?"

Natalie ignored Nate and sat at the table too. "I'll have Corn Flakes today, and Nicole will have the same thing."

"You know Nicole always has the cereal that makes the snap-crackle-and-pop noise," Bernadine said, so she poured Nicole a bowl of Rice Krispies.

"Oh, my," said Natalie, shaking her head, "I forgot my sneakers."

"Well, yell upstairs and tell your sister to bring them down and hurry up too," Bernadine said impatiently.

"Okay." Natalie closed her eyes real tight and put her hand to her forehead. She looked like she had a headache.

"What are you doing?" asked Nate.

Before Natalie could answer, Nicole skipped into the kitchen.

"Here's your sneakers, Natalie," she said. "But you didn't have to yell so loud."

Nate nearly knocked his bowl of cereal off the table. "I didn't hear anything. Did you?" he said, turning to Bernadine.

"No, I didn't. What are you *twins* up to?"

"Why, nothing," Natalie said.

14

"Of course you didn't hear anything. You're not a twin." Nicole dumped the Rice Krispies back into the box. "Hey, Natalie, I told you I wanted Corn Flakes today."

"I know. I heard you but Bernadine didn't believe me," Natalie sighed.

"Wait a minute," Bernadine asked suspiciously. "How come you twins didn't do this stuff before?"

15

"Maybe because we weren't old enough?" offered Nicole.

"Today is our birthday. That must be it!," Natalie exclaimed.

"Why, that means . . . ," Nate said.

"We can read each other's minds," the twins said together.

"Well, I don't believe it," Bernadine said. "And if we don't get moving, we'll miss the beginning of the movie." Just then Natalie jumped from her chair and ran up the stairs.

"Now what?" Bernadine sighed.

"Oh, she forgot her favorite bracelet," Nicole said casually.

When Natalie returned to the kitchen, she was fastening the bracelet on her wrist.

"Ready," Natalie said as she opened the back door.

"Let's go," said Nicole.

"No. It's impossible." Bernadine followed her sisters out the door. "I don't believe it."

"Oh, well. Have it your way," Natalie and Nicole said as one.

Bernadine's girlfriends were all at the movie theater.

"Baby-sitting the twins again?" chuckled Sandra.

Bernadine nodded and rolled her eyes at her twin sisters.

Nate and Natalie went looking for four seats while Bernadine and Nicole bought popcorn and candy.

"Over here, over here," Nate shouted.

"Did you bring me my chocolate-covered nuts?" Natalie asked.

Nicole handed the candy to her twin. "Yes, but next time think louder. It's noisy in here."

Nate's mouth dropped open but even he was too amazed to say a word.

When the matinee was over, everyone hurried out of the theater, blinking their eyes, trying to get used to the sunlight.

"Those were some movies, huh, twins?" Bernadine asked.

"Yeah, they were scary," Natalie answered.

"I wasn't scared a bit," Nate said. Natalie and Bernadine knew he wasn't telling the truth. He had held his hands over his eyes at the scary parts too.

"Hey, where's Nicole?" Bernadine asked.

Bernadine and Nate looked around, but there was only one twin. Like matching bookends it was odd to see one without the other.

"Maybe she's still inside. I'll look," Bernadine said. But a few minutes later she returned alone.

"If something's happened to her, I'm in big, big trouble," Bernadine cried. "And you too, Nate!"

"Hey, what did I do?" Nate asked.

"Well, I do know Nicole was upset when you told the ticket man that when you pinch one twin, the other twin will feel it too," Natalie said innocently enough.

"Yeah," Bernadine scolded. "You've been teasing the twins all day. You even said they walked like the alligator men in the movie."

"Well, you didn't tell me to stop," Nate scolded right back. "And besides, one of the twins is here."

"Well, maybe Nicole's more sensitive than Natalie. Maybe you hurt her feelings," Bernadine said. "Besides, I can't go home with just one!"

"Wait a minute," Nate beamed. "There's a simple solution for this."

"Oh? And what is that cousin?" Bernadine sighed.

"Why, all Natalie has to do is think real hard and ask Nicole where she is!" Nate offered.

"Yeah! You can read her mind," Bernadine added. "Like you did this morning."

"Just close your eyes and call out to Nicole. I'm sure she'll tell you where she is," Nate said.

Natalie looked at Nate then Bernadine. "I thought you didn't believe"

"I believe! I believe!" Nate and Bernadine cried.

Natalie closed her eyes tight. She looked like she had a headache. "Nicole is in the park." Without another word the frightened twosome grabbed Natalie and headed in that direction.

After a Saturday matinee the Murray Wricks Park was always crowded. So Natalie played on the swings while Nate and Bernadine looked everywhere—by the monkey bars, the basketball court, under the slide—but no Nicole. They walked unhappily back to the swings.

"She's not here," wailed Bernadine.

"Hey, what's up?" asked a voice behind them.

"Hey, Fish," Nate said. "Have you seen Natalie's other half?"

"Yeah, was she here?" Bernadine asked eagerly.

Fish casually took the end of his shirt and cleaned his glasses. "Nic was here a few minutes ago. She just left."

"Come on, Swami," Nate pleaded, turning to Natalie. "If you found Nicole once, you can find her again."

"Swami?" Natalie asked.

"He's a man I saw at the carnival last year who could see things in a crystal ball," Nate told her.

Natalie closed her eyes and rubbed her forehead. She looked like she had another headache. "Soda," she said. "Nicole's at Mrs. Anderson's grocery store buying a soda." Bernadine grabbed Natalie's hand, and they were off and running again.

While Bernadine and Nate walked up and down the aisles. Natalie leaned against the door, sipping a black cherry soda. Nate had bought the soda for her after she'd suggested it might help her find Nicole quicker.

"Looking for something?" Mrs. Anderson asked.

"Not something—someone," Nate said, sighing.

"We're looking for Nicole," Bernadine explained.

"Why, she was here a little while ago," Mrs. Anderson said. "She bought a soda, then left."

All of a sudden Bernadine and Nate perked up.

"Come on, Swami, try harder," Nate said.

"You've been right twice," Bernadine added. "Next time I'm sure we'll find her."

Natalie closed her eyes once again. This time she slowly turned in a circle with her arm outstretched and a finger pointing the direction.

"Nicole is at Grandma and Grandpa's," Natalie said. Bernadine and Nate ran out of the store, but Natalie just laughed to herself and finished her soda.

Bernadine beat Nate to their grandparents' doorstep and rang the buzzer.

"It's open," Grandpa said. "Come in."

Breathless. The two cousins ran into the house. And there was Nicole, sitting at Grandpa's side, eating ice cream. Fish was there too! Now what was he doing here?

"What took you so long?" Nicole asked.

"Well, we would've caught up with you long ago at the park," said Bernadine.

"Or at Mrs. Anderson's grocery store," said Nate. "If you had only waited for us."

"Why didn't you just tell Natalie in the beginning that you were going to end up here?" asked Bernadine wearily.

"Yeah, instead of leading us all over town?" asked Nate.

"But I did." Nicole revealed. I told Natalie this morning that I'd stop at the park first, then Mrs. Anderson's before meeting her here."

"This morning!" Nate and Bernadine shouted.

Just then Natalie walked into the room and looked at Nicole. The two sisters started to laugh.

"I wish you could have been there, Nic," Natalie said.

"Did they really follow you everywhere?" Nicole asked.

"Yes," Nat squealed. "Nate even bought me a soda so I'd find you faster."

"Hey, don't forget me," Fish added. "I did my part too." Grandpa, Nicole, and Fish laughed as Natalie told them everything that had happened. But Nate and Bernadine didn't laughed, and neither did Grandma.

Grandma looked at her two oldest grandchildren and shook her head. "You two should be ashamed of yourselves. Treating Natalie and Nicole like they're some freaks with special supernatural powers. They're just regular people like you. Only thing different is that they look alike and they were born a few minutes apart. But they're still two separate people."

Nate and Bernadine felt terrible.

"We're sorry, twins . . ."

"Who?" the twins asked.

"I mean Natalie and Nicole," Bernadine sighed.

"Yeah, you guys are okay," Nate added. "Honest."

"I guess we have been acting kinda silly," said Bernadine glumly. "You two sure gave us a birthday surprise."

"And it's not even your birthday," reminded Fish. "It's Natalie's and Nicole's."

"Well, I'm glad someone remembered who's birthday it is," Grandpa said.

"Bernadine, call your mom and dad and tell them we're starting the birthday party earlier than we'd planned."

Natalie peeked into the dining room and saw the cake and ice cream that Grandma had brought out.

"Wait . . . wait," Natalie said until she had everyone's attention. Then she slowly put her hand to her forehead and closed her eyes in thought. "I see birthday cake and chocolate, vanilla, and strawberry ice cream for everybody."

"Yes, O Swami," Nate said, bowing three times and pointing the way to the party.

"Yes, O Swami," they all repeated. And this time everybody laughed.

About the Author

Valerie Flournoy is the author of a number of well-known books for children including *The Patchwork Quilt*, which won the Coretta Scott King award for illustration, The Christopher Award, was an ALA Notable Children's Book, and was listed as an IRA-CBC Children's Choice Award.

Although Ms. Flournoy spends much of her time writing, she always manages to find the time to visit schools and speak to the students about the importance of education.

Ms. Flournoy lives in Palmyra, New Jersey. *The Twins Strike Back* is her first novel for Just Us Books.

About the Illustrator

Illustrator **Melodye Rosales** studied at The University of Illinois and the Universidad de Barcelona before continuing her studies at Columbia College and the Art Institute of Chicago.

Ms. Rosales has illustrated a number of picture books, including *Kwanzaa* and *Double Dutch and the Voodoo Shoes*, but lends her art to young adult jackets, as well. She also illustrated *Meet Addy* and other "Addy" titles in *The American Girls Collection*.

Ms. Rosales lives in Champaign, Illinois with her husband and three children.

The publisher wishes to extend special thanks to all the models who posed for the illustrations in this book: Kirstyn, Jillien, Eric, Stephan, LaTaeya, Sandy, Sonny, Curtis, Katura, and Mrs. Hazel Nimmo.